At the Bay

Katherine Mansfield

TABLE OF CONTENTS

Chapter I

VERY early morning. The sun was not yet risen, and the whole of Crescent Bay was hidden under a white sea-mist. The big bush-covered hills at the back were smothered. You could not see where they ended and the paddocks and bungalows be-gan. The sandy road was gone and the paddocks and bungalows the other side of it; there were no white dunes covered with reddish grass beyond them; there was nothing to mark which was beach and where was the sea. A heavy dew had fallen. The grass was blue. Big drops hung on the bushes and just did not fall; the silvery, fluffy toi-toi was limp on its long stalks, and all the marigolds and the pinks in the bungalow gardens were bowed to the earth with wetness. Drenched were the cold fuchsias, round pearls of dew lay on the flat nasturtium leaves. It looked as though the sea had beaten up softly in the darkness, as though one immense wave had come rippling, rippling – how far? Perhaps if you had waked up in the middle of the night you might have seen a big fish flicking in at the window and gone again. . . .

Ah-Aah! sounded the sleepy sea. And from the bush there came the sound of little streams flowing, quickly, lightly, slipping between the smooth stones, gushing into ferny basins and out again; and there was the splashing of big drops on large leaves, and something else – what was it? – a faint stirring and shaking, the snapping of a twig and then such silence that it seemed some one was listening.

Round the corner of Crescent Bay, between the piled-up masses of broken rock, a flock of sheep came pattering. They were huddled together, a small, tossing, woolly mass, and their thin, stick-like legs trotted along quickly as if the cold and the quiet had frightened them. Behind them an old sheepdog, his soaking paws covered with sand, ran along with his nose to the ground, but carelessly, as if thinking of something else. And then in the rocky gateway the shepherd himself appeared. He was a lean, upright old man, in a frieze coat that was covered with a web of tiny drops, velvet trousers tied under the knee, and a wide-awake with a folded blue handkerchief round the brim. One hand was crammed into his belt, the other grasped a beautifully smooth yellow stick. And as he walked, taking his time, he kept up a very soft light whistling, an airy, faraway fluting that sounded mournful and tender. The old dog cut an ancient caper or two and then drew up sharp, ashamed of his levity, and walked a few dignified paces by his master's side. The sheep ran forward in little pattering rushes; they began to bleat, and ghostly flocks and herds answered them from under the sea. "Baa! Baaa!" For a time they seemed to be always on the same piece of ground. There ahead was stretched the sandy road with shallow puddles; the same soaking bushes showed on either side and the same shadowy palings. Then something immense came into view; an enormous shock-haired giant with his arms stretched out. It was the big gum-tree outside Mrs. Stubbs' shop, and as they passed by there was a strong whiff of eucalyptus. And now big spots of light gleamed in the mist. The shepherd stopped whistling; he rubbed his red nose and wet beard on his wet sleeve and, screwing up his eyes, glanced in the direction of the sea. The sun was rising. It was marvellous how quickly the mist thinned, sped away, dissolved from the shallow plain, rolled up from the bush and was gone as if in a hurry to escape; big twists and curls jostled and shouldered each other as the silvery beams broadened. The faraway sky – a bright, pure blue-was reflected in the puddles, and the drops, swimming along the telegraph poles, flashed into points of light. Now the leaping, glittering sea was so bright it made one's eyes ache to look at it. The shepherd drew a pipe, the bowl as small as an acorn, out of his breast pocket, fumbled for a chunk of speckled tobacco, pared off a few shavings and stuffed the bowl. He was a grave, fine-looking old man. As he lit up and the blue smoke wreathed his head, the dog, watching, looked proud of him.

"Baa! Baaa!" The sheep spread out into a fan. They were just clear of the summer colony before the first sleeper turned over and lifted a drowsy head; their cry sounded in the dreams of little children . . . who lifted their arms to drag down, to cuddle the darling little woolly lambs of sleep. Then the first inhabitant appeared; it was the Burnells' cat Florrie, sitting on the gatepost, far too early as usual, looking for their milk-girl. When she saw the old sheepdog she sprang up quickly, arched her back, drew in her tabby head, and seemed to give a little fastidious shiver. "Ugh! What a coarse, revolting creature!" said Florrie. But the old sheepdog, not looking up, waggled past, flinging out his legs from side to side. Only one of his ears twitched to prove that he saw, and thought her a silly young female.

The breeze of morning lifted in the bush and the smell of leaves and wet black earth mingled with the sharp smell of the sea. Myriads of birds were singing. A goldfinch flew over the shepherd's head and, perching on the tiptop of a spray, it turned to the sun, ruffling its small breast feathers. And now they had passed the fisherman's hut, passed the charred-looking little whare where Leila the milk-girl lived with her old Gran. The sheep strayed over a yellow swamp and Wag, the sheep-dog, padded after, rounded them up and headed them for the steeper, narrower rocky pass that led out of Crescent Bay and towards Daylight Cove. "Baa! Baaa!" Faint the cry came as they rocked along the fast-drying road. The shepherd put away his pipe, dropping it into his breast-pocket so that the little bowl hung over. And straightway the soft airy whistling began again. Wag ran out along a ledge of rock after something that smelled, and ran back again disgusted. Then pushing, nudging, hurrying, the sheep rounded the bend and the shepherd followed after out of sight.

Chapter II

A few moments later the back door of one of the bungalows opened, and a figure in a broad-striped bathing suit flung down the paddock, cleared the stile, rushed through the tussock grass into the hollow, staggered up the sandy hillock, and raced for dear life over the big porous stones, over the cold, wet pebbles, on to the hard sand that gleamed like oil. Splish-Splosh! Splish-Splosh! The water bubbled round his legs as Stanley Burnell waded out exulting. First man in as usual! He'd beaten them all again. And he swooped down to souse his head and neck.

"Hail, brother! All hail, Thou Mighty One!" A velvety bass voice came booming over the water.

Great Scott! Damnation take it! Stanley lifted up to see a dark head bobbing far out and an arm lifted. It was Jonathan Trout – there before him! "Glorious morning!" sang the voice.

"Yes, very fine!" said Stanley briefly. Why the dickens didn't the fellow stick to his part of the sea? Why should he come barging over to this exact spot? Stanley gave a kick, a lunge and struck out, swimming overarm. But Jonathan was a match for him. Up he came, his black hair sleek on his forehead, his short beard sleek.

"I had an extraordinary dream last night!" he shouted.

What was the matter with the man? This mania for conversation irritated Stanley beyond words. And it was always the same – always some piffle about a dream he'd had, or some cranky idea he'd got hold of, or some rot he'd been reading. Stanley turned over on his back and kicked with his legs till he was a living water-spout. But even then . . . "I dreamed I was hanging over a terrifically high cliff, shouting to someone below." You would be! thought Stanley. He could stick no more of it. He stopped splashing. "Look here, Trout," he said, "I'm in rather a hurry this morning."

"You're WHAT?" Jonathan was so surprised – or pretended to be – that he sank under the water, then reappeared again blowing.

"All I mean is," said Stanley, "I've no time to – to – to fool about. I want to get this over. I'm in a hurry. I've work to do this morning – see?"

Jonathan was gone before Stanley had finished. "Pass, friend!" said the bass voice gently, and he slid away through the water with scarcely a ripple . . . But curse the fellow! He'd ruined Stanley's bathe. What an unpractical idiot the man was! Stanley struck out to sea again, and then as quickly swam in again, and away he rushed up the beach. He felt cheated.

Jonathan stayed a little longer in the water. He floated, gently moving his hands like fins, and letting the sea rock his long, skinny body. It was curious, but in spite of everything he was fond of Stanley Burnell. True, he had a fiendish desire to tease him sometimes, to poke fun at him, but at bottom he was sorry for the fellow. There was something pathetic in his determination to make a job of everything. You couldn't help feeling he'd be caught out one day, and then what an almighty cropper he'd come! At that moment an immense wave lifted Jonathan, rode past him, and broke along the beach with a joyful sound. What a beauty! And now there came another. That was the way to live – carelessly, recklessly, spending oneself. He got on to his feet and began to wade towards the shore, pressing his toes into the firm, wrinkled sand. To take things easy, not to fight against the ebb and flow of life, but to give way to it – that was what was needed. It was this tension that was all wrong. To live – to live! And the perfect morning, so fresh and fair, basking in the light, as though laughing at its own beauty, seemed to whisper, "Why not?"

But now he was out of the water Jonathan turned blue with cold. He ached all over; it was as though someone was wringing the blood out of him. And stalking up the beach, shivering, all his muscles tight, he too felt his bathe was spoilt. He'd stayed in too long.

Chapter III

Beryl was alone in the living-room when Stanley appeared, wearing a blue serge suit, a stiff collar and a spotted tie. He looked almost uncannily clean and brushed; he was going to town for the day. Dropping into his chair, he pulled out his watch and put it beside his plate.

"I've just got twenty-five minutes," he said. "You might go and see if the porridge is ready, Beryl?"

"Mother's just gone for it," said Beryl. She sat down at the table and poured out his tea.

"Thanks!" Stanley took a sip. "Hallo!" he said in an astonished voice, "you've forgotten the sugar."

"Oh, sorry!" But even then Beryl didn't help him; she pushed the basin across. What did this mean? As Stanley helped himself his blue eyes widened; they seemed to quiver. He shot a quick glance at his sister-in-law and leaned back.

"Nothing wrong, is there?" he asked carelessly, fingering his collar.

Beryl's head was bent; she turned her plate in her fingers.

"Nothing," said her light voice. Then she too looked up, and smiled at Stanley. "Why should there be?"

"O-oh! No reason at all as far as I know. I thought you seemed rather – "

At that moment the door opened and the three little girls appeared, each carrying a porridge plate. They were dressed alike in blue jerseys and knickers; their brown legs were bare, and each had her hair plaited and pinned up in what was called a horse's tail. Behind them came Mrs. Fairfield with the tray.

"Carefully, children," she warned. But they were taking the very greatest care. They loved being allowed to carry things. "Have you said good morning to your father?"

"Yes, grandma." They settled themselves on the bench opposite Stanley and Beryl.

"Good morning, Stanley!" Old Mrs. Fairfield gave him his plate.

"Morning, mother! How's the boy?"

"Splendid! He only woke up once last night. What a perfect morning!" The old woman paused, her hand on the loaf of bread, to gaze out of the open door into the garden. The sea sounded. Through the wide-open window streamed the sun on to the yellow varnished walls and bare floor. Everything on the table flashed and glittered. In the middle there was an old salad bowl filled with yellow and red nasturtiums. She smiled, and a look of deep content shone in her eyes.

"You might cut me a slice of that bread, mother," said Stanley. "I've only twelve and a half minutes before the coach passes. Has anyone given my shoes to the servant girl?"

"Yes, they're ready for you." Mrs. Fairfield was quite unruffled.

"Oh, Kezia! Why are you such a messy child!" cried Beryl despairingly.

"Me, Aunt Beryl?" Kezia stared at her. What had she done now? She had only dug a river down the middle of her porridge, filled it, and was eating the banks away. But she did that every single morning, and no one had said a word up till now.

"Why can't you eat your food properly like Isabel and Lottie?" How unfair grownups are!

"But Lottie always makes a floating island, don't you, Lottie?"

"I don't," said Isabel smartly. "I just sprinkle mine with sugar and put on the milk and finish it. Only babies play with their food."

Stanley pushed back his chair and got up.

"Would you get me those shoes, mother? And, Beryl, if you've finished, I wish you'd cut down to the gate and stop the coach. Run in to your mother, Isabel, and ask her where my bowler hat's been put. Wait a minute – have you children been playing with my stick?"

"No, father!"

But I put it here," Stanley began to bluster. "I remember distinctly putting it in this corner. Now, who's had it? There's no time to lose. Look sharp! The stick's got to be found."

Even Alice, the servant-girl, was drawn into the chase. "You haven't been using it to poke the kitchen fire with by any chance?"

Stanley dashed into the bedroom where Linda was lying. "Most extraordinary thing. I can't keep a single possession to myself. They've made away with my stick, now!"

"Stick, dear? What stick?" Linda's vagueness on these occasions could not be real, Stanley decided. Would nobody sympathize with him?

"Coach! Coach, Stanley!" Beryl's voice cried from the gate.

Stanley waved his arm to Linda. "No time to say Goodbye!" he cried. And he meant that as a punishment to her.

He snatched his bowler hat, dashed out of the house, and swung down the garden path. Yes, the coach was there waiting, and Beryl, leaning over the open gate, was laughing up at somebody or other just as if nothing had happened. The heartlessness of women! The way they took it for granted it was your job to slave away for them while they didn't even take the trouble to see that your walking-stick wasn't lost. Kelly trailed his whip across the horses.

"Goodbye, Stanley," called Beryl, sweetly and gaily. It was easy enough to say Goodbye! And there she stood, idle, shading her eyes with her hand. The worst of it was Stanley had to shout Goodbye too, for the sake of appearances. Then he saw her turn, give a little skip and run back to the house. She was glad to be rid of him!

Yes, she was thankful. Into the living-room she ran and called "He's gone!" Linda cried from her room: "Beryl! Has Stanley gone?" Old Mrs. Fairfield appeared, carrying the boy in his little flannel coatee.

"Gone?"

"Gone!"

Oh, the relief, the difference it made to have the man out of the house. Their very voices were changed as they called to one another; they sounded warm and loving and as if they shared a secret. Beryl went over to the table. "Have another cup of tea, mother. It's still hot." She wanted, somehow, to celebrate the fact that they could do what they liked now. There was no man to disturb them; the whole perfect day was theirs.

"No, thank you, child," said old Mrs. Fairfield, but the way at that moment she tossed the boy up and said "a-goos-a-goos-a-ga!" to him meant that she felt the same. The little girls ran into the paddock like chickens let out of a coop.

Even Alice, the servant-girl, washing up the dishes in the kitchen, caught the infection and used the precious tank water in a perfectly reckless fashion.

"Oh, these men!" said she, and she plunged the teapot into the bowl and held it under the water even after it had stopped bubbling, as if it too was a man and drowning was too good for them.

Chapter IV

"Wait for me, Isabel! Kezia, wait for me!"

There was poor little Lottie, left behind again, because she found it so fearfully hard to get over the stile by herself. When she stood on the first step her knees began to wobble; she grasped the post. Then you had to put one leg over. But which leg? She never could decide. And when she did finally put one leg over with a sort of stamp of despair – then the feeling was awful. She was half in the paddock still and half in the tussock grass. She clutched the post desperately and lifted up her voice. "Wait for me!"

"No, don't you wait for her, Kezia!" said Isabel. "She's such a little silly. She's always making a fuss. Come on!" And she tugged Kezia's jersey. "You can use my bucket if you come with me," she said kindly. "It's bigger than yours." But Kezia couldn't leave Lottie all by herself. She ran back to her. By this time Lottie was very red in the face and breathing heavily.

"Here, put your other foot over," said Kezia.

"Where?"

Lottie looked down at Kezia as if from a mountain height.

"Here where my hand is." Kezia patted the place.

"Oh, there do you mean!" Lottie gave a deep sigh and put the second foot over.

"Now – sort of turn round and sit down and slide," said Kezia.

"But there's nothing to sit down on, Kezia," said Lottie.

She managed it at last, and once it was over she shook herself and began to beam.

"I'm getting better at climbing over stiles, aren't I, Kezia?"

Lottie's was a very hopeful nature.

The pink and the blue sunbonnet followed Isabel's bright red sunbonnet up that sliding, slipping hill. At the top they paused to decide where to go and to have a good stare at who was there already. Seen from behind, standing against the skyline, gesticulating largely with their spades, they looked like minute puzzled explorers.

The whole family of Samuel Josephs was there already with their lady-help, who sat on a camp-stool and kept order with a whistle that she wore tied round her neck, and a small cane with which she directed operations. The Samuel Josephs never played by themselves or managed their own game. If they did, it ended in the boys pouring water down the girls' necks or the girls trying to put little black crabs into the boys' pockets. So Mrs. S. J. and the poor lady-help drew up what she called a "brogramme" every morning to keep them "abused and out of bischief." It was all competitions or races or round games. Everything began with a piercing blast of the lady-help's whistle and ended with another. There were even prizes — large, rather dirty paper parcels which the lady-help with a sour little smile drew out of a bulging string kit. The Samuel Josephs fought fearfully for the prizes and cheated and pinched one another's arms — they were all expert pinchers. The only time the Burnell children ever played with them Kezia had got a prize, and when she undid three bits of paper she found a very small rusty buttonhook. She couldn't understand why they made such a fuss.

. . .

But they never played with the Samuel Josephs now or even went to their parties. The Samuel Josephs were always giving children's parties at the Bay and there was always the same food. A big washhand basin of very brown fruit-salad, buns cut into four and a washhand jug full of something the lady-help called "Limonadear." And you went away in the evening with half the frill torn off your frock or something spilled all down the front of your openwork pinafore, leaving the Samuel Josephs leaping like savages on their lawn. No! They were too awful.

On the other side of the beach, close down to the water, two little boys, their knickers rolled up, twinkled like spiders. One was digging, the other pattered in and out of the water, filling a small bucket. They were the Trout boys, Pip and Rags. But Pip was so busy digging and Rags was so busy helping that they didn't see their little cousins until they were quite close.

"Look!" said Pip. "Look what I've discovered."
And he showed them an old wet, squashed-
looking boot. The three little girls stared.

"Whatever are you going to do with it?" asked
Kezia.

"Keep it, of course!" Pip was very scornful.
"It's a find – see?"

Yes, Kezia saw that. All the same. . .

"There's lots of things buried in the sand,"
explained Pip. "They get chucked up from
wrecks. Treasure. Why – you might find – "

"But why does Rags have to keep on pouring
water in?" asked Lottie.

"Oh, that's to moisten it," said Pip, "to make
the work a bit easier. Keep it up, Rags."

And good little Rags ran up and down, pouring
in the water that turned brown like cocoa.

"Here, shall I show you what I found yester-day?" said Pip mysteriously, and he stuck his spade into the sand. "Promise not to tell."

They promised.

"Say, cross my heart straight dinkum."

The little girls said it.

Pip took something out of his pocket, rubbed it a long time on the front of his jersey, then breathed on it and rubbed it again.

"Now turn round!" he ordered.

They turned round.

"All look the same way! Keep still! Now!"

And his hand opened; he held up to the light something that flashed, that winked, that was a most lovely green.

"It's a nemeral," said Pip solemnly.

"Is it really, Pip?" Even Isabel was impressed.

The lovely green thing seemed to dance in Pip's fingers. Aunt Beryl had a nemeral in a ring, but it was a very small one. This one was as big as a star and far more beautiful.

Chapter V

As the morning lengthened whole parties appeared over the sand-hills and came down on the beach to bathe. It was understood that at eleven o'clock the women and children of the summer colony had the sea to themselves. First the women undressed, pulled on their bathing dresses and covered their heads in hideous caps like sponge bags; then the children were unbuttoned. The beach was strewn with little heaps of clothes and shoes; the big summer hats, with stones on them to keep them from blowing away, looked like immense shells. It was strange that even the sea seemed to sound differently when all those leaping, laughing figures ran into the waves. Old Mrs. Fairfield, in a lilac cotton dress and a black hat tied under the chin, gathered her little brood and got them ready. The little Trout boys whipped their shirts over their heads, and away the five sped, while their grandma sat with one hand in her knitting-bag ready to draw out the ball of wool when she was satisfied they were safely in.

The firm compact little girls were not half so brave as the tender, delicate-looking boys. Pip and Rags, shivering, crouching down, slapping the water, never hesitated. But Isabel, who could swim twelve strokes, and Kezia, who could nearly swim eight, only followed on the strict understanding they were not to be splashed. As for Lottie, she didn't follow at all. She liked to be left to go in her own way, please. And that way was to sit down at the edge of the water, her legs straight, her knees pressed together, and to make vague motions with her arms as if she expected to be wafted out to sea. But when a bigger wave than usual, an old whiskery one, came lolloping along in her direction, she scrambled to her feet with a face of horror and flew up the beach again.

"Here, mother, keep those for me, will you?"

Two rings and a thin gold chain were dropped into Mrs Fairfield's lap.

"Yes, dear. But aren't you going to bathe here?"

"No-o," Beryl drawled. She sounded vague. "I'm undressing farther along. I'm going to bathe with Mrs. Harry Kember."

"Very well." But Mrs. Fairfield's lips set. She disapproved of Mrs Harry Kember. Beryl knew it.

Poor old mother, she smiled, as she skimmed over the stones. Poor old mother! Old! Oh, what joy, what bliss it was to be young. . . .

"You look very pleased," said Mrs. Harry Kember. She sat hunched up on the stones, her arms round her knees, smoking.

"It's such a lovely day," said Beryl, smiling down at her.

"Oh my dear! "Mrs. Harry Kember's voice sounded as though she knew better than that. But then her voice always sounded as though she knew something more about you than you did yourself. She was a long, strange-looking woman with narrow hands and feet. Her face, too, was long and narrow and exhausted-looking; even her fair curled fringe looked burnt out and withered. She was the only woman at the Bay who smoked, and she smoked incessantly, keeping the cigarette between her lips while she talked, and only taking it out when the ash was so long you could not understand why it did not fall. When she was not playing bridge – she played bridge every day of her life – she spent her time lying in the full glare of the sun. She could stand any amount of it; she never had enough. All the same, it did not seem to warm her. Parched, withered, cold, she stretched on the stones like a piece of tossed-up driftwood. The women at the Bay thought she was very, very fast. Her lack of vanity, her slang, the way she treated men as though she was one of them, and the fact that she didn't care twopence about her house and called the servant Gladys "Glad-eyes," was disgraceful. Standing on the veranda steps Mrs. Kember would call in her indifferent, tired voice, "I say, Glad-eyes, you might heave me a handkerchief if I've got one, will you?" And Glad-eyes, a red bow in her hair instead of a cap, and white shoes, came running with an impudent smile. It was an absolute scandal! True, she had no children, and her husband. . . . Here the voices were always raised; they became fervent. How can he have married her? How can he, how can he? It must have been money, of course, but even then!

Mrs. Kember's husband was at least ten years younger than she was, and so incredibly handsome that he looked like a mask or a most perfect illustration in an American novel rather than a man. Black hair, dark blue eyes, red lips, a slow sleepy smile, a fine tennis player, a perfect dancer, and with it all a mystery. Harry Kember was like a man walking in his sleep. Men couldn't stand him, they couldn't get a word out of the chap; he ignored his wife just as she ignored him. How did he live? Of course there were stories, but such stories! They simply couldn't be told. The women he's been seen with, the places he'd been seen in . . . but nothing was ever certain, nothing definite. Some of the women at the Bay privately thought he'd commit a murder one day. Yes, even while they talked to Mrs. Kember and took in the awful concoction she was wearing, they saw her, stretched as she lay on the beach; but cold, bloody, and still with a cigarette stuck in the corner of her mouth.

Mrs. Kember rose, yawned, unsnapped her belt buckle, and tugged at the tape of her blouse. And Beryl stepped out of her skirt and shed her jersey, and stood up in her short white petticoat, and her camisole with ribbon bows on the shoulders.

"Mercy on us," said Mrs. Harry Kember, "what a little beauty you are!"

"Don't!" said Beryl softly; but, drawing off one stocking and then the other, she felt a little beauty.

"My dear – why not?" said Mrs. Harry Kember, stamping on her own petticoat. Really – her underclothes! A pair of blue cotton knickers and a linen bodice that reminded one somehow of a pillowcase. . . . "And you don't wear stays, do you?" She touched Beryl's waist, and Beryl sprang away with a small affected cry. Then "Never!" she said firmly.

"Lucky little creature," sighed Mrs. Kember, unfastening her own.

Beryl turned her back and began the complicated movements of someone who is trying to take off her clothes and to pull on her bathing-dress all at one and the same time.

"Oh, my dear – don't mind me," said Mrs. Harry Kember. "Why be shy? I shan't eat you. I shan't be shocked like those other ninnies." And she gave her strange neighing laugh and grimaced at the other women.

But Beryl was shy. She never undressed in front of anybody. Was that silly? Mrs. Harry Kember made her feel it was silly, even something to be ashamed of. Why be shy indeed! She glanced quickly at her friend standing so boldly in her torn chemise and lighting a fresh cigarette; and a quick, bold, evil feeling started up in her breast. Laughing recklessly, she drew on the limp, sandy-feeling bathing-dress that was not quite dry and fastened the twisted buttons.

"That's better," said Mrs. Harry Kember. They began to go down the beach together. "Really, it's a sin for you to wear clothes, my dear. Somebody's got to tell you some day."

The water was quite warm. It was that marvellous transparent blue, flecked with silver, but the sand at the bottom looked gold; when you kicked with your toes there rose a little puff of gold-dust. Now the waves just reached her breast. Beryl stood, her arms outstretched, gazing out, and as each wave came she gave the slightest little jump, so that it seemed it was the wave which lifted her so gently.

"I believe in pretty girls having a good time," said Mrs. Harry Kember. "Why not? Don't you make a mistake, my dear. Enjoy yourself." And suddenly she turned turtle, disappeared, and swam away quickly, quickly, like a rat. Then she flicked round and began swimming back. She was going to say something else. Beryl felt that she was being poisoned by this cold woman, but she longed to hear. But oh, how strange, how horrible! As Mrs. Harry Kember came up close she looked, in her black waterproof bathing-cap, with her sleepy face lifted above the water, just her chin touching, like a horrible caricature of her husband.

Chapter VI

In a steamer chair, under a manuka tree that grew in the middle of the front grass patch, Linda Burnell dreamed the morning away. She did nothing. She looked up at the dark, close, dry leaves of the manuka, at the chinks of blue between, and now and again a tiny yellowish flower dropped on her. Pretty – yes, if you held one of those flowers on the palm of your hand and looked at it closely, it was an exquisite small thing. Each pale yellow petal shone as if each was the careful work of a loving hand. The tiny tongue in the centre gave it the shape of a bell. And when you turned it over the outside was a deep bronze colour. But as soon as they flowered, they fell and were scattered. You brushed them off your frock as you talked; the horrid little things got caught in one's hair. Why, then, flower at all? Who takes the trouble – or the joy – to make all these things that are wasted, wasted. . . . It was uncanny.

On the grass beside her, lying between two pillows, was the boy. Sound asleep he lay, his head turned away from his mother. His fine dark hair looked more like a shadow than like real hair, but his ear was a bright, deep coral. Linda clasped her hands above her head and crossed her feet. It was very pleasant to know that all these bungalows were empty, that everybody was down on the beach, out of sight, out of hearing. She had the garden to herself; she was alone.

Dazzling white the picotees shone; the golden-eyed marigold glittered; the nasturtiums wreathed the veranda poles in green and gold flame. If only one had time to look at these flowers long enough, time to get over the sense of novelty and strangeness, time to know them! But as soon as one paused to part the petals, to discover the underside of the leaf, along came Life and one was swept away. And, lying in her cane chair, Linda felt so light; she felt like a leaf. Along came Life like a wind and she was seized and shaken; she had to go. Oh dear, would it always be so? Was there no escape?

. . . Now she sat on the veranda of their Tasmanian home, leaning against her father's knee. And he promised, "As soon as you and I are old enough, Linny, we'll cut off somewhere, we'll escape. Two boys together. I have a fancy I'd like to sail up a river in China." Linda saw that river, very wide, covered with little rafts and boats. She saw the yellow hats of the boatmen and she heard their high, thin voices as they called . . .

"Yes, papa."

But just then a very broad young man with bright ginger hair walked slowly past their house, and slowly, solemnly even, uncovered. Linda's father pulled her ear teasingly, in the way he had.

"Linny's beau," he whispered.

"Oh, papa, fancy being married to Stanley Burnell!"

Well, she was married to him. And what was more she loved him. Not the Stanley whom everyone saw, not the everyday one; but a timid, sensitive, innocent Stanley who knelt down every night to say his prayers, and who longed to be good. Stanley was simple. If he believed in people – as he believed in her, for instance – it was with his whole heart. He could not be disloyal; he could not tell a lie. And how terribly he suffered if he thought anyone – she – was not being dead straight, dead sincere with him! "This is too subtle for me!" He flung out the words, but his open quivering, distraught look was like the look of a trapped beast.

But the trouble was – here Linda felt almost inclined to laugh, though Heaven knows it was no laughing matter – she saw her Stanley so seldom. There were glimpses, moments, breathing spaces of calm, but all the rest of the time it was like living in a house that couldn't be cured of the habit of catching on fire, on a ship that got wrecked every day. And it was always Stanley who was in the thick of the danger. Her whole time was spent in rescuing him, and restoring him, and calming him down, and listening to his story. And what was left of her time was spent in the dread of having children.

Linda frowned; she sat up quickly in her steamer chair and clasped her ankles. Yes, that was her real grudge against life; that was what she could not understand. That was the question she asked and asked, and listened in vain for the answer. It was all very well to say it was the common lot of women to bear children. It wasn't true. She, for one, could prove that wrong. She was broken, made weak, her courage was gone, through childbearing. And what made it doubly hard to bear was, she did not love her children. It was useless pretending. Even if she had had the strength she never would have nursed and played with the little girls. No, it was as though a cold breath had chilled her through and through on each of those awful journeys; she had no warmth left to give them. As to the boy – well, thank Heaven, mother had taken him; he was mother's, or Beryl's, or anybody's who wanted him. She had hardly held him in her arms. She was so indifferent about him that as he lay there . . . Linda glanced down.

The boy had turned over. He lay facing her, and he was no longer asleep. His dark-blue, baby eyes were open; he looked as though he was peeping at his mother. And suddenly his face dimpled; it broke into a wide, toothless smile, a perfect beam, no less.

"I'm here!" that happy smile seemed to say. "Why don't you like me?"

There was something so quaint, so unexpected about that smile that Linda smiled herself. But she checked herself and said to the boy coldly, "I don't like babies."

"Don't like babies?" The boy couldn't believe her. "Don't like me? "He waved his arms foolishly at his mother.

Linda dropped off her chair on to the grass.

"Why do you keep on smiling?" she said severely. "If you knew what I was thinking about, you wouldn't."

But he only squeezed up his eyes, slyly, and rolled his head on the pillow. He didn't believe a word she said.

"We know all about that!" smiled the boy.

Linda was so astonished at the confidence of this little creature. . . . Ah no, be sincere. That was not what she felt; it was something far different, it was something so new, so . . . The tears danced in her eyes; she breathed in a small whisper to the boy, "Hallo, my funny!"

But by now the boy had forgotten his mother. He was serious again. Something pink, something soft waved in front of him. He made a grab at it and it immediately disappeared. But when he lay back, another, like the first, appeared. This time he determined to catch it. He made a tremendous effort and rolled right over.

Chapter VII

The tide was out; the beach was deserted; lazily flopped the warm sea. The sun beat down, beat down hot and fiery on the fine sand, baking the grey and blue and black and white-veined pebbles. It sucked up the little drop of water that lay in the hollow of the curved shells; it bleached the pink convolvulus that threaded through and through the sand-hills. Nothing seemed to move but the small sand-hoppers. Pit-pit-pit! They were never still.

Over there on the weed-hung rocks that looked at low tide like shaggy beasts come down to the water to drink, the sunlight seemed to spin like a silver coin dropped into each of the small rock pools. They danced, they quivered, and minute ripples laved the porous shores. Looking down, bending over, each pool was like a lake with pink and blue houses clustered on the shores; and oh! the vast mountainous country behind those houses – the ravines, the passes, the dangerous creeks and fearful tracks that led to the water's edge. Underneath waved the sea-forest – pink threadlike trees, velvet anemones, and orange berry-spotted weeds. Now a stone on the bottom moved, rocked, and there was a glimpse of a black feeler; now a threadlike creature wavered by and was lost. Something was happening to the pink, waving trees; they were changing to a cold moonlight blue. And now there sounded the faintest "plop." Who made that sound? What was going on down there? And how strong, how damp the seaweed smelt in the hot sun. . . .

The green blinds were drawn in the bungalows of the summer colony. Over the verandas, prone on the paddock, flung over the fences, there were exhausted-looking bathing-dresses and rough striped towels. Each back window seemed to have a pair of sandshoes on the sill and some lumps of rock or a bucket or a collection of pawa shells. The bush quivered in a haze of heat; the sandy road was empty except for the Trouts' dog Snooker, who lay stretched in the very middle of it. His blue eye was turned up, his legs stuck out stiffly, and he gave an occasional desperate-sounding puff, as much as to say he had decided to make an end of it and was only waiting for some kind cart to come along.

"What are you looking at, my grandma? Why do you keep stopping and sort of staring at the wall?"

Kezia and her grandmother were taking their siesta together. The little girl, wearing only her short drawers and her under-bodice, her arms and legs bare, lay on one of the puffed-up pillows of her grandma's bed, and the old woman, in a white ruffled dressing-gown sat in a rocker at the window, with a long piece of pink knitting in her lap. This room that they shared, like the other rooms of her bungalow, was of light varnished wood and the floor was bare. The furniture was of the shabbiest, the simplest. The dressing-table, for instance, was a packing-case in a sprigged muslin petticoat, and the mirror above was very strange; it was as though a little piece of forked lightning was imprisoned in it. On the table there stood a jar of sea-pinks, pressed so tightly together they looked more like a velvet pincushion, and a special shell which Kezia had given her grandma for a pin-tray, and another even more special which she had thought would make a very nice place for a watch to curl up in.

"Tell me, grandma," said Kezia.

The old woman sighed, whipped the wool twice round her thumb, and drew the bone needle through. She was casting on.

"I was thinking of your Uncle William, darling," she said quietly.

"My Australian Uncle William?" said Kezia. She had another.

"Yes, of course."

"The one I never saw?"

"That was the one."

"Well, what happened to him?" Kezia knew perfectly well, but she wanted to be told again.

"He went to the mines, and he got a sunstroke there and died," said old Mrs. Fairfield.

Kezia blinked and considered the picture again . . . a little man fallen over like a tin soldier by the side of the big black hole.

"Does it make you sad to think about him, grandma?" She hated her grandma to be sad.

It was the old woman's turn to consider. Did it make her sad? To look back, back. To stare down the years, as Kezia had seen her doing. To look after them as a woman does, long after they were out of sight. Did it make her sad? No, life was like that.

"No, Kezia."

"But why?" asked Kezia. She lifted one bare arm and began to draw things in the air. "Why did Uncle William have to die? He wasn't old."

Mrs. Fairfield began counting the stitches in threes. "It just happened," she said in an absorbed voice.

"Does everybody have to die?" asked Kezia.

"Everybody!"

"Me? "Kezia sounded fearfully incredulous.

"Some day, my darling."

"But, grandma." Kezia waved her left leg and waggled the toes. They felt sandy. "What if I just won't?"

The old woman sighed again and drew a long thread from the ball.

"We're not asked, Kezia," she said sadly. "It happens to all of us sooner or later."

Kezia lay still thinking this over. She didn't want to die. It meant she would have to leave here, leave everywhere, for ever, leave – leave her grandma. She rolled over quickly.

"Grandma," she said in a startled voice.

"What, my pet!"

"You're not to die." Kezia was very decided.

"Ah, Kezia" – her grandma looked up and smiled and shook her head – "don't let's talk about it."

"But you're not to. You couldn't leave me. You couldn't not be there." This was awful. "Promise me you won't ever do it, grandma," pleaded Kezia.

The old woman went on knitting.

"Promise me! Say never!"

But still her grandma was silent.

Kezia rolled off her bed; she couldn't bear it any longer, and lightly she leapt on to her grandma's knees, clasped her hand round the old woman's throat and began kissing her, under the chin, behind the ear, and blowing down her neck.

"Say never . . . say never . . . say never – " She gasped between the kisses. And then she began, very softly and lightly, to tickle her grandma.

"Kezia!" The old woman dropped her knitting. She swung back in the rocker. She began to tickle Kezia. "Say never, say never, say never," gurgled Kezia, while they lay there laughing in each other's arms. "Come, that's enough, my squirrel! That's enough, my wild pony!" said old Mrs. Fairfield, setting her cap straight. "Pick up my knitting."

Both of them had forgotten what the "never" was about.

Chapter VIII

The sun was still full on the garden when the back door of the Burnells' shut with a bang, and a very gay figure walked down the path to the gate. It was Alice, the servant-girl, dressed for her afternoon out. She wore a white cotton dress with such large red spots on it and so many that they made you shudder, white shoes and a leghorn turned up under the brim with poppies. Of course she wore gloves, white ones, stained at the fastenings with ironmould, and in one hand she carried a very dashed-looking sunshade which she referred to as her perishall.

Beryl, sitting in the window, fanning her freshly-washed hair, thought she had never seen such a guy. If Alice had only blacked her face with a piece of cork before she started out, the picture would have been complete. And where did a girl like that go to in a place like this? The heart-shaped Fijian fan beat scornfully at that lovely bright mane. She supposed Alice had picked up some horrible common larrikin and they'd go off into the bush together. Pity to have made herself so conspicuous; they'd have hard work to hide with Alice in that rig-out.

But no, Beryl was unfair. Alice was going to tea with Mrs Stubbs, who'd sent her an "invite" by the little boy who called for orders. She had taken ever such a liking to Mrs. Stubbs ever since the first time she went to the shop to get something for her mosquitoes.

"Dear heart!" Mrs. Stubbs had clapped her hand to her side. "I never seen anyone so eaten. You might have been attacked by canningbals."

Alice did wish there'd been a bit of life on the road though. Made her feel so queer, having nobody behind her. Made her feel all weak in the spine. She couldn't believe that someone wasn't watching her. And yet it was silly to turn round; it gave you away. She pulled up her gloves, hummed to herself and said to the distant gum-tree, "Shan't be long now." But that was hardly company.

Mrs. Stubbs's shop was perched on a little hillock just off the road. It had two big windows for eyes, a broad veranda for a hat, and the sign on the roof, scrawled MRS. STUBBS'S, was like a little card stuck rakishly in the hat crown.

On the veranda there hung a long string of bathing-dresses, clinging together as though they'd just been rescued from the sea rather than waiting to go in, and beside them there hung a cluster of sandshoes so extraordinarily mixed that to get at one pair you had to tear apart and forcibly separate at least fifty. Even then it was the rarest thing to find the left that belonged to the right. So many people had lost patience and gone off with one shoe that fitted and one that was a little too big. . . . Mrs. Stubbs prided herself on keeping something of everything. The two windows, arranged in the form of precarious pyramids, were crammed so tight, piled so high, that it seemed only a conjurer could prevent them from toppling over. In the left-hand corner of one window, glued to the pane by four gelatine lozenges, there was – and there had been from time immemorial – a notice.

LOST! HANSOME GOLE BROOCH

SOLID GOLD

ON OR NEAR BEACH

REWARD OFFERED

Alice pressed open the door. The bell jangled, the red serge curtains parted, and Mrs. Stubbs appeared. With her broad smile and the long bacon knife in her hand, she looked like a friendly brigand. Alice was welcomed so warmly that she found it quite difficult to keep up her "manners." They consisted of persistent little coughs and hems, pulls at her gloves, tweaks at her skirt, and a curious difficulty in seeing what was set before her or understanding what was said.

Tea was laid on the parlour table – ham, sardines, a whole pound of butter, and such a large johnny cake that it looked like an advertisement for somebody's baking-powder. But the Primus stove roared so loudly that it was useless to try to talk above it. Alice sat down on the edge of a basket-chair while Mrs. Stubbs pumped the stove still higher. Suddenly Mrs. Stubbs whipped the cushion off a chair and disclosed a large brown-paper parcel.

"I've just had some new photers taken, my dear," she shouted cheerfully to Alice. "Tell me what you think of them."

In a very dainty, refined way Alice wet her finger and put the tissue back from the first one. Life! How many there were! There were three dozzing at least. And she held it up to the light.

Mrs. Stubbs sat in an armchair, leaning very much to one side. There was a look of mild astonishment on her large face. and well there might be. For though the armchair stood on a carpet, to the left of it, miraculously skirting the carpet-border, there was a dashing water-fall. On her right stood a Grecian pillar with a giant fern-tree on either side of it, and in the background towered a gaunt mountain, pale with snow.

"It is a nice style, isn't it?" shouted Mrs. Stubbs; and Alice had just screamed "Sweetly" when the roaring of the Primus stove died down, fizzled out, ceased, and she said "Pretty" in a silence that was frightening.

"Draw up your chair, my dear," said Mrs. Stubbs, beginning to pour out. "Yes," she said thoughtfully, as she handed the tea, "but I don't care about the size. I'm having an enlargemint. All very well for Christmas cards, but I never was the one for small photers myself. You get no comfort out of them. To say the truth, I find them dis'eartening."

Alice quite saw what she meant.

"Size," said Mrs. Stubbs. "Give me size. That was what my poor dear husband was always saying. He couldn't stand anything small. Gave him the creeps. And, strange as it may seem my dear" – here Mrs. Stubbs creaked and seemed to expand herself at the memory – "it was dropsy that carried him off at the larst. Many's the time they drawn one and a half pints from 'im at the 'ospital . . . It seemed like a judgemint."

Alice burned to know exactly what it was that was drawn from him. She ventured, "I suppose it was water."

But Mrs. Stubbs fixed Alice with her eyes and replied meaningly, "It was liquid, my dear."

Liquid! Alice jumped away from the word like a cat and came back to it, nosing and wary.

"That's 'im!" said Mrs. Stubbs, and she pointed dramatically to the life-size head and shoulders of a burly man with a dead white rose in the buttonhole of his coat that made you think of a curl of cold mutting fat. Just below, in silver letters on a red cardboard ground, were the words, "Be not afraid, it is I."

"It's ever such a fine face," said Alice faintly.

The pale-blue bow on the top of Mrs. Stubbs's fair frizzy hair quivered. She arched her plump neck. What a neck she had! It was bright pink where it began and then it changed to warm apricot, and that faded to the colour of a brown egg and then to a deep creamy.

"All the same, my dear," she said surprisingly, "freedom's best!" Her soft, fat chuckle sounded like a purr. "Freedom's best," said Mrs. Stubbs again.

Freedom! Alice gave a loud, silly little titter. She felt awkward. Her mind flew back to her own kitching. Ever so queer! She wanted to be back in it again.

Chapter IX

A strange company assembled in the Burnells' washhouse after tea. Round the table there sat a bull, a rooster, a donkey that kept forgetting it was a donkey, a sheep and a bee. The washhouse was the perfect place for such a meeting because they could make as much noise as they liked, and nobody ever interrupted. It was a small tin shed standing apart from the bungalow. Against the wall there was a deep trough and in the corner a copper with a basket of clothes-pegs on top of it. The little window, spun over with cobwebs, had a piece of candle and a mousetrap on the dusty sill. There were clotheslines crisscrossed overhead and, hanging from a peg on the wall, a very big, a huge, rusty horseshoe. The table was in the middle with a form at either side.

"You can't be a bee, Kezia. A bee's not an animal. It's a ninseck."

"Oh, but I do want to be a bee frightfully," wailed Kezia. . . . A tiny bee, all yellow-furry, with striped legs. She drew her legs up under her and leaned over the table. She felt she was a bee.

"A ninseck must be an animal," she said stoutly. "It makes a noise. It's not like a fish."

"I'm a bull, I'm a bull!" cried Pip. And he gave such a tremendous bellow – how did he make that noise? – that Lottie looked quite alarmed.

"I'll be a sheep," said little Rags. "A whole lot of sheep went past this morning."

"How do you know?"

"Dad heard them. Baa!" He sounded like the little lamb that trots behind and seems to wait to be carried.

"Cock-a-doodle-do!" shrilled Isabel. With her red cheeks and bright eyes she looked like a rooster.

"What'll I be?" Lottie asked everybody, and she sat there smiling, waiting for them to decide for her. It had to be an easy one.

"Be a donkey, Lottie." It was Kezia's suggestion. "Hee-haw! You can't forget that."

"Hee-haw!" said Lottie solemnly. "When do I have to say it?"

"I'll explain, I'll explain," said the bull. It was he who had the cards. He waved them round his head. "All be quiet! All listen!" And he waited for them. "Look here, Lottie." He turned up a card. "It's got two spots on it – see? Now, if you put that card in the middle and somebody else has one with two spots as well, you say 'Hee-haw,' and the card's yours."

"Mine?" Lottie was round-eyed. "To keep?"

"No, silly. Just for the game, see? Just while we're playing." The bull was very cross with her.

"Oh, Lottie, you are a little silly," said the proud rooster.

Lottie looked at both of them. Then she hung her head; her lip quivered. "I don't want to play," she whispered. The others glanced at one another like conspirators. All of them knew what that meant. She would go away and be discovered somewhere standing with her pinny thrown over her head, in a corner, or against a wall, or even behind a chair.

"Yes, you do, Lottie. It's quite easy," said Kezia.

And Isabel, repentant, said exactly like a grownup, "Watch me , Lottie, and you'll soon learn."

"Cheer up, Lot," said Pip. "There, I know what I'll do. I'll give you the first one. It's mine, really, but I'll give it to you. Here you are." And he slammed the card down in front of Lottie.

Lottie revived at that. But now she was in another difficulty. "I haven't got a hanky," she said; "I want one badly, too."

"Here, Lottie, you can use mine." Rags dipped into his sailor blouse and brought up a very wet-looking one, knotted together. "Be very careful," he warned her. "Only use that corner. Don't undo it. I've got a little starfish inside I'm going to try and tame."

"Oh, come on, you girls," said the bull. "And mind – you're not to look at your cards. You've got to keep your hands under the table till I say 'Go.'"

Smack went the cards round the table. They tried with all their might to see, but Pip was too quick for them. It was very exciting, sitting there in the washhouse; it was all they could do not to burst into a little chorus of animals before Pip had finished dealing.

"Now, Lottie, you begin."

Timidly Lottie stretched out a hand, took the top card off her pack, had a good look at it – it was plain she was counting the spots – and put it down.

"No, Lottie, you can't do that. You mustn't look first. You must turn it the other way over."

"But then everybody will see it the same time as me," said Lottie. The game proceeded. Mooe-ooo-er! The bull was terrible. He charged over the table and seemed to eat the cards up.

Bss-ss! said the bee.

Cock-a-doodle-do! Isabel stood up in her excitement and moved her elbows like wings.

Baa! Little Rags put down the King of Diamonds and Lottie put down the one they called the King of Spain. She had hardly any cards left.

"Why don't you call out, Lottie?"

"I've forgotten what I am," said the donkey woefully.

"Well, change! Be a dog instead! Bow-wow!"

"Oh yes. That's much easier." Lottie smiled again. But when she and Kezia both had a one Kezia waited on purpose. The others made signs to Lottie and pointed. Lottie turned very red; she looked bewildered, and at last she said, "Hee-haw! Ke-zia."

"Ss! Wait a minute!" They were in the very thick of it when the bull stopped them, holding up his hand. "What's that? What's that noise?"

"What noise? What do you mean?" asked the rooster.

"Ss! Shut up! Listen!" They were mouse-still. "I thought I heard a – a sort of knocking," said the bull.

"What was it like?" asked the sheep faintly.

No answer.

The bee gave a shudder. "Whatever did we shut the door for?" she said softly. Oh, why, why had they shut the door?

While they were playing, the day had faded; the gorgeous sunset had blazed and died. And now the quick dark came racing over the sea, over the sand-hills, up the paddock. You were frightened to look in the corners of the washhouse, and yet you had to look with all your might. And somewhere, far away, grandma was lighting a lamp. The blinds were being pulled down; the kitchen fire leapt in the tins on the mantelpiece.

"It would be awful now," said the bull, "if a spider was to fall from the ceiling on to the table, wouldn't it?"

"Spiders don't fall from ceilings."

"Yes, they do. Our Min told us she'd seen a spider as big as a saucer, with long hairs on it like a gooseberry."

Quickly all the little heads were jerked up; all the little bodies drew together, pressed together.

"Why doesn't somebody come and call us?" cried the rooster.

Oh, those grownups, laughing and snug, sitting in the lamplight, drinking out of cups! They'd forgotten about them. No, not really forgotten. That was what their smile meant. They had decided to leave them there all by themselves.

Suddenly Lottie gave such a piercing scream that all of them jumped off the forms, all of them screamed too. "A face – a face looking!" shrieked Lottie.

It was true, it was real. Pressed against the window was a pale face, black eyes, a black beard.

"Grandma! Mother! Somebody!"

But they had not got to the door, tumbling over one another, before it opened for Uncle Jonathan. He had come to take the little boys home.

Chapter X

He had meant to be there before, but in the front garden he had come upon Linda walking up and down the grass, stopping to pick off a dead pink or give a top-heavy carnation something to lean against, or to take a deep breath of something, and then walking on again, with her little air of remoteness. Over her white frock she wore a yellow, pink-fringed shawl from the Chinaman's shop.

"Hallo, Jonathan!" called Linda. And Jonathan whipped off his shabby panama, pressed it against his breast, dropped on one knee, and kissed Linda's hand.

"Greeting, my Fair One! Greeting, my Celestial Peach Blossom!" boomed the bass voice gently. "Where are the other noble dames?"

"Beryl's out playing bridge and mother's giving the boy his bath. . . . Have you come to borrow something?"

The Trouts were for ever running out of things and sending across to the Burnells' at the last moment.

But Jonathan only answered, "A little love, a little kindness;" and he walked by his sister-in-law's side.

Linda dropped into Beryl's hammock under the manuka tree, and Jonathan stretched himself on the grass beside her, pulled a long stalk and began chewing it. They knew each other well. The voices of children cried from the other gardens. A fisherman's light cart shook along the sandy road, and from far away they heard a dog barking; it was muffled as though the dog had its head in a sack. If you listened you could just hear the soft swish of the sea at full tide sweeping the pebbles. The sun was sinking.

"And so you go back to the office on Monday, do you, Jonathan?" asked Linda.

"On Monday the cage door opens and clangs to upon the victim for another eleven months and a week," answered Jonathan.

Linda swung a little. "It must be awful," she said slowly.

"Would ye have me laugh, my fair sister? Would ye have me weep?"

Linda was so accustomed to Jonathan's way of talking that she paid no attention to it.

"I suppose," she said vaguely, "one gets used to it. One gets used to anything."

"Does one? Hum!" the "Hum" was so deep it seemed to boom from underneath the ground. "I wonder how it's done," brooded Jonathan; "I've never managed it."

Looking at him as he lay there, Linda thought again how attractive he was. It was strange to think that he was only an ordinary clerk, that Stanley earned twice as much money as he. What was the matter with Jonathan? He had no ambition; she supposed that was it. And yet one felt he was gifted, exceptional. He was passionately fond of music; every spare penny he had went on books. He was always full of new ideas, schemes, plans. But nothing came of it all. The new fire blazed in Jonathan; you almost heard it roaring softly as he explained, described and dilated on the new thing; but a moment later it had fallen in and there was nothing but ashes, and Jonathan went about with a look like hunger in his black eyes. At these times he exaggerated his absurd manner of speaking, and he sang in church – he was the leader of the choir – with such fearful dramatic intensity that the meanest hymn put on an unholy splendour.

"It seems to me just as imbecile, just as infernal, to have to go to the office on Monday," said Jonathan, "as it always has done and always will do. To spend all the best years of one's life sitting on a stool from nine to five, scratching in somebody's ledger! It's a queer use to make of one's . . . one and only life, isn't it? Or do I fondly dream?" He rolled over on the grass and looked up at Linda. "Tell me, what is the difference between my life and that of an ordinary prisoner? The only difference I can see is that I put myself in jail and nobody's ever going to let me out. That's a more intolerable situation than the other. For if I'd been – pushed in, against my will – kicking, even – once the door was locked, or at any rate in five years or so, I might have accepted the fact and begun to take an interest in the flight of flies or counting the warder's steps along the passage with particular attention to variations of tread and so on. But as it is, I'm like an insect that's flown into a room of its own accord. I dash against the walls, dash against the windows, flop against the ceiling, do everything on God's earth, in fact, except fly out again. And all the while I'm thinking, like that moth, or that butterfly, or whatever it is, 'The shortness of life! The shortness of life!' I've only one night or one day, and there's this vast dangerous garden, waiting out there, undiscovered, unexplored."

"But, if you feel like that, why – " began Linda quickly.

"Ah! "cried Jonathan. And that "ah!" was somehow almost exultant. There you have me. Why? Why indeed? There's the maddening, mysterious question. Why don't I fly out again? There's the window or the door or whatever it was I came in by. It's not hopelessly shut – is it? Why don't I find it and be off? Answer me that, little sister." But he gave her no time to answer.

"I'm exactly like that insect again. For some reason" – Jonathan paused between the words – "it's not allowed, it's forbidden, it's against the insect law, to stop banging and flopping and crawling up the pane even for an instant. Why don't I leave the office? Why don't I seriously consider, this moment, for instance, what it is that prevents me leaving? It's not as though I'm tremendously tied. I've two boys to provide for, but, after all, they're boys. I could cut off to sea, or get a job upcountry, or – " Suddenly he smiled at Linda and said in a changed voice, as if he were confiding a secret, "Weak . . . weak. No stamina. No anchor. No guiding principle, let us call it." But then the dark velvety voice rolled out:"

Would ye hear the story
How it unfolds itself . . .

and they were silent.

The sun had set. In the western sky there were great masses of crushed-up rose-coloured clouds. Broad beams of light shone through the clouds and beyond them as if they would cover the whole sky. Overhead the blue faded; it turned a pale gold, and the bush outlined against it gleamed dark and brilliant like metal. Sometimes when those beams of light show in the sky they are very awful. They remind you that up there sits Jehovah, the jealous God, the Almighty, Whose eye is upon you, ever watchful, never weary. You remember that at His coming the whole earth will shake into one ruined graveyard; the cold, bright angels will drive you this way and that, and there will be no time to explain what could be explained so simply. . . . But tonight it seemed to Linda there was something infinitely joyful and loving in those silver beams. And now no sound came from the sea. It breathed softly as if it would draw that tender, joyful beauty into its own bosom.

"It's all wrong, it's all wrong," came the shadowy voice of Jonathan. "It's not the scene, it's not the setting for . . . three stools, three desks, three ink pots and a wire blind."

Linda knew that he would never change, but she said, "Is it too late, even now?"

"I'm old – I'm old," intoned Jonathan. He bent towards her, he passed his hand over his head. "Look!" His black hair was speckled all over with silver, like the breast plumage of a black fowl.

Linda was surprised. She had no idea that he was grey. And yet, as he stood up beside her and sighed and stretched, she saw him, for the first time, not resolute, not gallant, not careless, but touched already with age. He looked very tall on the darkening grass, and the thought crossed her mind, "He is like a weed."

Jonathan stooped again and kissed her fingers.

"Heaven reward thy sweet patience, lady mine," he murmured. "I must go seek those heirs to my fame and fortune. . . ." He was gone.

Chapter XI

Light shone in the windows of the bungalow. Two square patches of gold fell upon the pinks and the peaked marigolds. Florrie, the cat, came out on to the veranda, and sat on the top step, her white paws close together, her tail curled round. She looked content, as though she had been waiting for this moment all day.

"Thank goodness, it's getting late," said Florrie. "Thank goodness, the long day is over." Her greengage eyes opened.

Presently there sounded the rumble of the coach, the crack of Kelly's whip. It came near enough for one to hear the voices of the men from town, talking loudly together. It stopped at the Burnells' gate.

Stanley was halfway up the path before he saw Linda. "Is that you, darling?"

"Yes, Stanley."

He leapt across the flowerbed and seized her in his arms. She was enfolded in that familiar, eager, strong embrace.

"Forgive me, darling, forgive me," stammered Stanley, and he put his hand under her chin and lifted her face to him.

"Forgive you?" smiled Linda. "But whatever for?"

"Good God! You can't have forgotten," cried Stanley Burnell. "I've thought of nothing else all day. I've had the hell of a day. I made up my mind to dash out and telegraph, and then I thought the wire mightn't reach you before I did. I've been in tortures, Linda."

"But, Stanley," said Linda, "what must I forgive you for?"

"Linda!" – Stanley was very hurt – "didn't you realize – you must have realized – I went away without saying Goodbye to you this morning? I can't imagine how I can have done such a thing. My confounded temper, of course. But – well"

– and he sighed and took her in his arms again – "I've suffered for it enough today."

"What's that you've got in your hand?" asked Linda. "New gloves? Let me see."

"Oh, just a cheap pair of wash-leather ones," said Stanley humbly. "I noticed Bell was wearing some in the coach this morning, so, as I was passing the shop, I dashed in and got myself a pair. What are you smiling at? You don't think it was wrong of me, do you?"

"On the contrary, darling," said Linda, "I think it was most sensible."

She pulled one of the large, pale gloves on her own fingers and looked at her hand, turning it this way and that. She was still smiling.

Stanley wanted to say, "I was thinking of you the whole time I bought them." It was true, but for some reason he couldn't say it. "Let's go in," said he.

Chapter XII

Why does one feel so different at night? Why is it so exciting to be awake when everybody else is asleep? Late – it is very late! And yet every moment you feel more and more wakeful, as though you were slowly, almost with every breath, waking up into a new, wonderful, far more thrilling and exciting world than the daylight one. And what is this queer sensation that you're a conspirator? Lightly, stealthily you move about your room. You take something off the dressing-table and put it down again without a sound. And everything, even the bedpost, knows you, responds, shares your secret. . . .

You're not very fond of your room by day. You never think about it. You're in and out, the door opens and slams, the cupboard creaks. You sit down on the side of your bed, change your shoes and dash out again. A dive down to the glass, two pins in your hair, powder your nose and off again. But now – it's suddenly dear to you. It's a darling little funny room. It's yours. Oh, what a joy it is to own things! Mine – my own!

"My very own for ever?"

"Yes." Their lips met.

No, of course, that had nothing to do with it. That was all nonsense and rubbish. But, in spite of herself, Beryl saw so plainly two people standing in the middle of her room. Her arms were round his neck; he held her. And now he whispered, "My beauty, my little beauty!" She jumped off her bed, ran over to the window and kneeled on the window-seat, with her elbows on the sill. But the beautiful night, the garden, every bush, every leaf, even the white palings, even the stars, were conspirators too. So bright was the moon that the flowers were bright as by day; the shadow of the nasturtiums, exquisite lily-like leaves and wide-open flowers, lay across the silvery veranda. The manuka-tree, bent by the southerly winds, was like a bird on one leg stretching out a wing.

But when Beryl looked at the bush, it seemed to her the bush was sad.

"We are dumb trees, reaching up in the night, imploring we know not what," said the sorrowful bush.

It is true when you are by yourself and you think about life, it is always sad. All that excitement and so on has a way of suddenly leaving you, and it's as though, in the silence, somebody called your name, and you heard your name for the first time. "Beryl!"

"Yes, I'm here. I'm Beryl. Who wants me?"

"Beryl!"

"Let me come."

It is lonely living by oneself. Of course, there are relations, friends, heaps of them; but that's not what she means. She wants someone who will find the Beryl they none of them know, who will expect her to be that Beryl always. She wants a lover.

Take me away from all these other people, my love. Let us go far away. Let us live our life, all new, all ours, from the very beginning. Let us make our fire. Let us sit down to eat together. Let us have long talks at night."

And the thought was almost, "Save me, my love. Save me!"

. . . "Oh, go on! Don't be a prude, my dear. You enjoy yourself while you're young. That's my advice." And a high rush of silly laughter joined Mrs. Harry Kember's loud, indifferent neigh.

You see, it's so frightfully difficult when you've nobody. You're so at the mercy of things. You can't just be rude. And you've always this horror of seeming inexperienced and stuffy like the other ninnies at the Bay. And – and it's fascinating to know you've power over people. Yes, that is fascinating. . . .

Oh why, oh why doesn't "he" come soon?

If I go on living here, thought Beryl, anything may happen to me.

"But how do you know he is coming at all?" mocked a small voice within her.

But Beryl dismissed it. She couldn't be left. Other people, perhaps, but not she. It wasn't possible to think that Beryl Fairfield never married, that lovely fascinating girl.

"Do you remember Beryl Fairfield?"

"Remember her! As if I could forget her! It was one summer at the Bay that I saw her. She was standing on the beach in a blue" – no, pink – "muslin frock, holding on a big cream" – no, black – "straw hat. But it's years ago now."

"She's as lovely as ever, more so if anything."

Beryl smiled, bit her lip, and gazed over the garden. As she gazed, she saw somebody, a man, leave the road, step along the paddock beside their palings as if he was coming straight towards her. Her heart beat. Who was it? Who could it be? It couldn't be a burglar, certainly not a burglar, for he was smoking and he strolled lightly. Beryl's heart leapt; it seemed to turn right over, and then to stop. She recognized him.

"Good evening, Miss Beryl," said the voice softly.

"Good evening."

"Won't you come for a little walk?" it drawled.

Come for a walk – at that time of night! "I couldn't. Everybody's in bed. Everybody's asleep."

"Oh," said the voice lightly, and a whiff of sweet smoke reached her. "What does everybody matter? Do come! It's such a fine night. There's not a soul about."

Beryl shook her head. But already something stirred in her, something reared its head.

The voice said, "Frightened?" It mocked, "Poor little girl!"

"Not in the least," said she. As she spoke that weak thing within her seemed to uncoil, to grow suddenly tremendously strong; she longed to go!

And just as if this was quite understood by the other, the voice said, gently and softly, but finally, "Come along!"

Beryl stepped over her low window, crossed the veranda, ran down the grass to the gate. He was there before her.

"That's right," breathed the voice, and it teased, "You're not frightened, are you? You're not frightened?"

She was; now she was here she was terrified, and it seemed to her everything was different. The moonlight stared and glittered; the shadows were like bars of iron. Her hand was taken.

"Not in the least," she said lightly. "Why should I be?"

Her hand was pulled gently, tugged. She held back.

"No, I'm not coming any farther," said Beryl.

"Oh, rot!" Harry Kember didn't believe her. "Come along! We'll just go as far as that fuchsia bush. Come along!"

The fuchsia bush was tall. It fell over the fence in a shower. There was a little pit of darkness beneath.

"No, really, I don't want to," said Beryl.

For a moment Harry Kember didn't answer. Then he came close to her, turned to her, smiled and said quickly, "Don't be silly! Don't be silly!"

His smile was something she'd never seen before. Was he drunk? That bright, blind, terrifying smile froze her with horror. What was she doing? How had she got here? the stern garden asked her as the gate pushed open, and quick as a cat Harry Kember came through and snatched her to him.

"Cold little devil! Cold little devil!" said the hateful voice.

But Beryl was strong. She slipped, ducked, wrenched free.

"You are vile, vile," said she.

"Then why in God's name did you come?" stammered Harry Kember.

Nobody answered him.

Chapter XIII

A cloud, small, serene, floated across the moon. In that moment of darkness the sea sounded deep, troubled. Then the cloud sailed away, and the sound of the sea was a vague murmur, as though it waked out of a dark dream. All was still.

www.ReadHowYouWant.com

You can buy our **Large Type** and **EasyRead** books from our www.ReadHowYouWant.com website, from websites like Amazon.com and through your UK and North American bookshop.

EasyRead books are designed to make your reading easy and enjoyable. **EasyRead** books are published in different font sizes, so you can select the font size best for you.

EasyRead is for people with normal eyesight who want books in an easy-to-read format.

EasyRead Comfort is for people who find reading small print tiring but do not need large print.

EasyRead Large is for people who find it easier to read larger print.

EasyRead Large Bold is for people with retinal problems who need to read high contrast text.

EasyRead Super Large is for people who require large and dense format, available in 18pt, 20pt and 24pt.

The **EasyRead** font, character, word and line spacing have all been set to make it as easy as possible both to recognize a word, and to run your eye along a line of text without losing your place. We split as few words as possible at line ends, as split words make reading harder and can be annoying. For out-of-copyright books, words have been changed to modern spelling (where the sense is not affected), and the original hyphenation of compound words has been retained where this improves word recognition or sense.

With most things you buy, you get a choice, and you can choose the make and model that suits best. There is a big exception – books. You don't get to choose a format that is easy for you to read – you have to read the format the publisher selects.

This "**One Size Fits All**" paradigm **no longer** need apply to books.

At www.ReadHowYouWant.com, you can order a book just as you want it, so you can read it easily. You can choose nearly any format, and at a surprisingly low cost, because of a technical breakthrough that allows us to typeset an individual book automatically, print and bind the book and have it quickly sent directly to you.

You can have your book in **Talking Book** formats **(DAISY or MP3)** or as an **E-book** or in **Braille**.

We have developed totally new visual formats which we hope will help people with **dyslexia** and other print reading disabilities. Look at www.ReadHowYouWant.com for more information.

Good news for publishers and authors. There is a big market for large type, personalized and accessible format books. We can help publishers and authors find new market opportunities for their books, and selling your book through www.ReadHowYouWant.com is easy – we do the work for you. Contact us on info@ReadHowYouWant.com.